The Super Adventures of
OLLIE
AND
BEA

SQUEALS ON WHEELS

Here's Bea and her best friend, Oll—

HEY! WAIT A MINUTE!
WHERE'S OLLIE?

RENÉE TREML

PICTURE WINDOW BOOKS
a capstone imprint

Published by Picture Window Books, an imprint of Capstone.
1710 Roe Crest Drive, North Mankato, Minnesota 56003
capstonepub.com

Library of Congress Cataloging-in-Publication Data
Names: Treml, Renée, author. | Treml, Renée, author.
Title: Squeals on wheels / Renée Treml.
Description: North Mankato, Minnesota : Picture Window Books, [2022] | Series: The super adventures of Ollie and Bea | Audience: Ages 5-7 | Audience: Grades K-1 |
Summary: "Ollie is having a hoot on his roller skates-but Bea is full of excuses for why she can not join in. Will Bea realize that real friends do not mind if you sometimes look silly?"-- Provided by publisher.
Identifiers: LCCN 2021043789 (print) | LCCN 2021043790 (ebook) | ISBN 9781666314892 (hardcover) | ISBN 9781666330915 (paperback) | ISBN 9781666330922 (pdf) | ISBN 9781666330946 (kindle edition)
Subjects: CYAC: Graphic novels. | Humorous stories. | Owls--Fiction. | Rabbits--Fiction. | Friendship--Fiction. | LCGFT: Funny animal comics. | Graphic novels.
Classification: LCC PZ7.7.T73 Sq 2022 (print) | LCC PZ7.7.T73 (ebook) | DDC 741.5/994--dc23
LC record available at https://lccn.loc.gov/2021043789
LC ebook record available at https://lccn.loc.gov/2021043790

Designed by Kay Fraser

TABLE OF CONTENTS

CHAPTER 1
OWL BE BACK

Have you seen Ollie?

4

I'm right here, Bea!

Oh.

Hey! What's black and white and has sixteen wheels?

I have no idea.

A ZEBRA ON ROLLER SKATES!

What are you doing, Ollie?

Besides making a **spectacle** of myself?

Well, I wasn't going to say anything . . .

6

Have you forgotten that we're skating today?

NO . . .

but I wasn't going to say anything about that, either.

7

Don't worry! I don't know how either. I'm just winging it!

Uh-huh.

Ooof! It's a lot of fun.

Looks like it.

8

I know, right?

Hey, Bea. Do you know what the hardest part of skating is?

Balance?

Coordination?

THE GROUND!
But that's why we wear
a helmet!

C'mon! Get your skates.
Everyone is waiting for you.

You go on ahead. I'll
be right behind you.

You brought your
skates today, right?

10

Um . . . of course.
We all know how
much I love doing
stuff that involves
my big feet.

GREAT!
Put them on.
Owl be back
really soon.

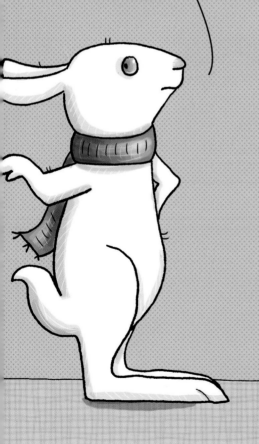

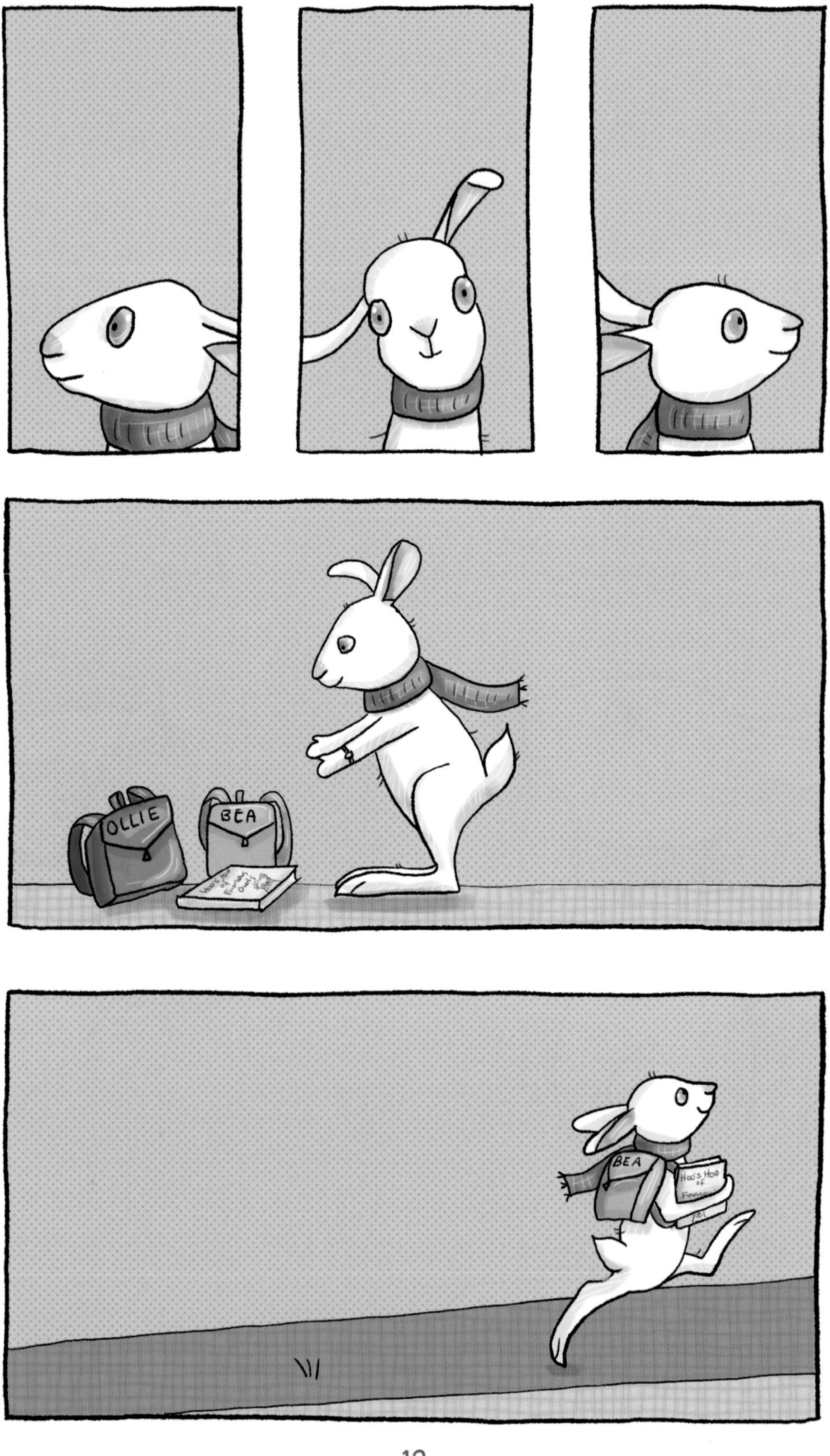
OLLIE
BEA
BEA

I'm back, Bea.

Bea?

Hey! Where'd she go?

Hoo's Hoo of Famous Owls

BEA

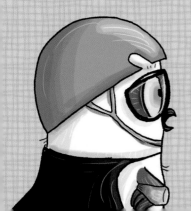

13

CHAPTER 2
HOP TO IT

BEA! BEA! OVER HERE!

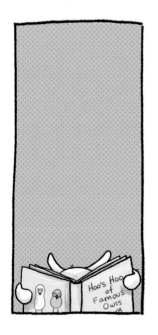

Are you reading my **_Hoo's Hoo of Famous Owls?_**

Oh, yes. I *love, love, love* boring stuff. I find it . . . uh . . . fascinating.

14

Wow! I didn't know you liked owl history too. But aren't we skating today?

We are . . . but I can't stop until I finish this chapter. It's a real cliff-hanger.

You skate on ahead and I'll catch up with you in a bit.

15

Hey! I've got a great joke.
Knock, knock.

Who's there?

Canoe.

CANOE WHO?

16

CANOE help me with my owl history?

HA! HA! That's funny, Bea. Now what were we talking about?

I'm being serious. Let's sit down right now and you tell me all about this really boring book.

17

Oh, now I remember!
We're skating!

Where are your skates?
Are they in your bag?

No. Yes.
I don't know.

Great! Where'd
your bag go?

Oops. I must
have left it
at home.

BEA

Really?

Yes. Why don't you go back to skating and I'll run home and—

Silly rabbit! It's right here behind you. Maybe you need glasses too.

OH, CARROT STICKS!

Look at that. They aren't in here. And I was SO sure I brought them today. Oh well.

Do you know what this means?

Yep, I can't skate today.

NO . . . THIS IS A MYSTERY!

I wouldn't call this a "mystery"—

But your skates have disappeared and you don't know where they are. **We'll call it a RIDDLE instead!**

Well, to be honest, they aren't exactly missing—

We'll need the Super Team to help!

No, we don't need—

22

HEY, SUPER TEAM! WE'VE GOT A RIDDLE TO SOLVE!

Not really a riddle either . . .

CHAPTER 3
MY *DEER* FRIENDS

Hey, Ollie!

Hi, Bea!

OH NO!
GET *OTTER* THE WAY!

24

Oh, *deer.*

Are you okay?

Yes!

THIS IS THE MOST FUN EVER!

So, what's up, muchachos?

25

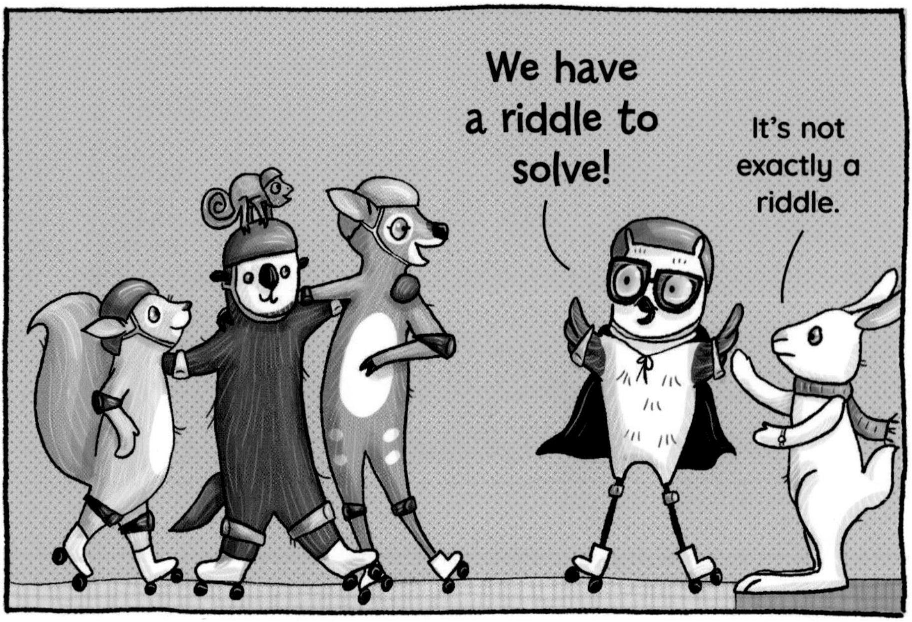
We have a riddle to solve!
It's not exactly a riddle.

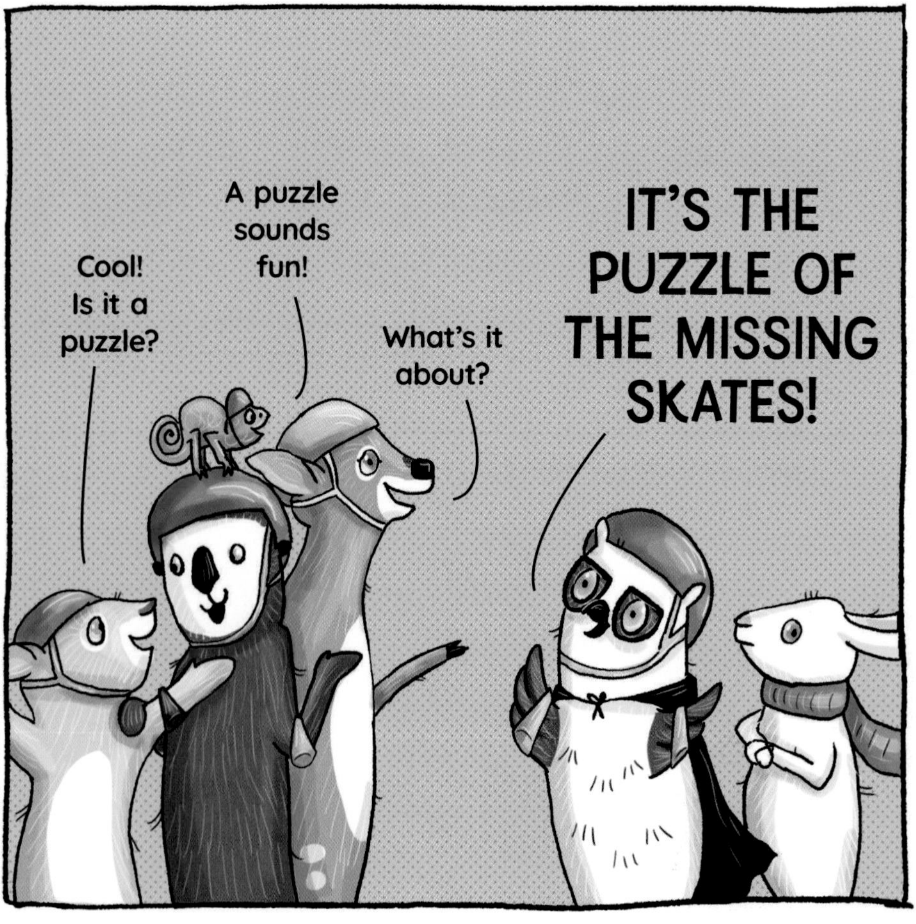
Cool! Is it a puzzle?
A puzzle sounds fun!
What's it about?
IT'S THE PUZZLE OF THE MISSING SKATES!

We'll find them!

Where did you see them last?

Oh, wow! That's terrible!

Well . . . like I said before . . . uh . . . well . . . they aren't exactly . . . and I . . .

27

Okay, team. Let's search for the missing skates.

We won't stop until we find them!

We'll check over here.

I'll stay with Bea and try to cheer her up. She is so sad about her missing skates.

Don't worry, Bea. The team will keep looking as long as it takes. Even if it takes all day and no one gets to skate.

WAIT!

EVERYONE COME BACK!

29

You should go back to skating. I don't need my skates. I'll be fine watching.

Don't be silly, Bea. We're a Super Team! We'll solve this puzzle together!

I tried to tell you. There is no mystery or riddle or puzzle.

30

Sure there is!

Your skates are missing.

And we don't know where they are!

My skates aren't missing.

I didn't bring them.

You should go have fun.

I'll be here.

Reading this really boring book.

Hoo's Hoo of Famous Owls

31

Super Team, we'll meet up with you in a bit.

I HAVE A SUPERPLAN!

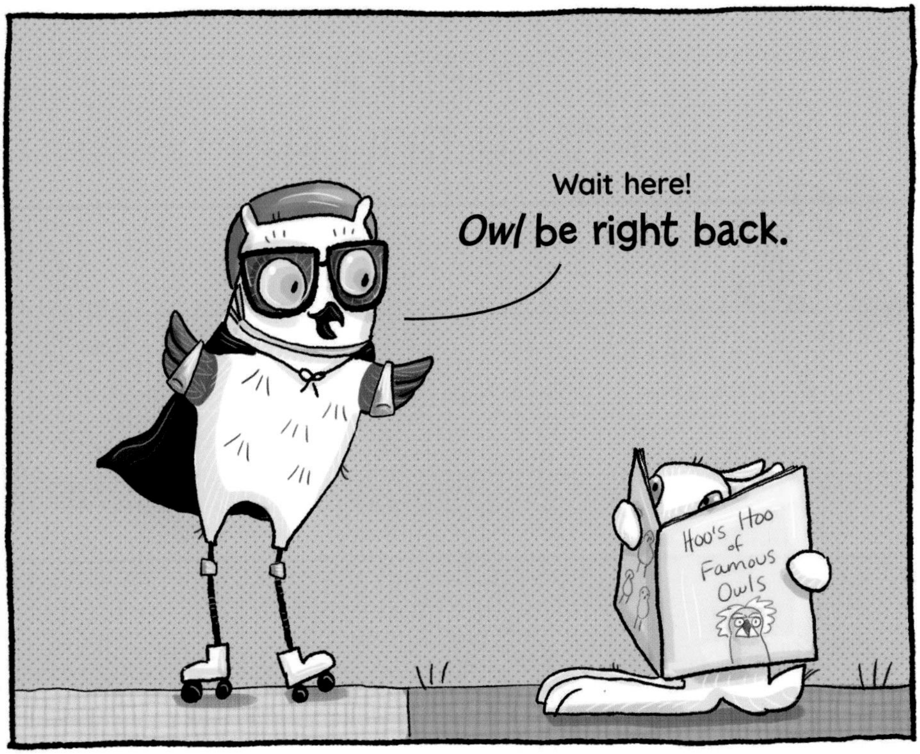
Wait here!
Owl be right back.
Hoo's Hoo of Famous Owls

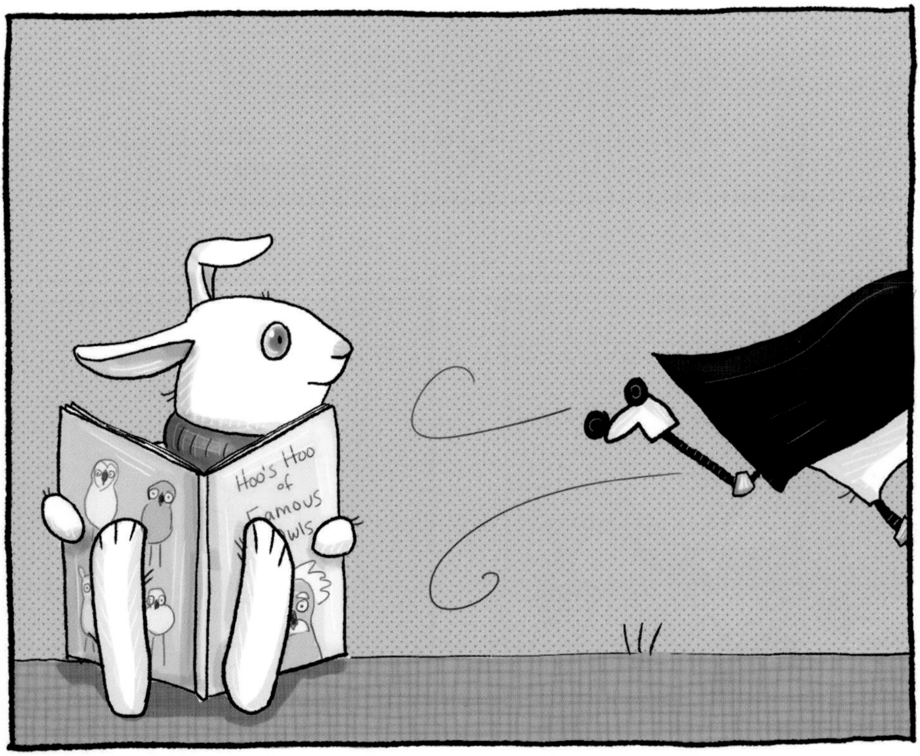
Hoo's Hoo of Famous Owls

CHAPTER 4
POLAR ROLLERS

Here, these are for you. I borrowed them from our teacher.

I don't think they will fit.

34

Sure they will!

OUR TEACHER IS
A GIGANTIC
POLAR BEAR.

**THEY WILL
DEFINITELY FIT!**

Did you feel that? It's starting to rain. We better get inside.

But Bea, there's not a cloud in the sky.

Did you hear that? My mom is calling.

I don't hear a thing.

That helmet must be blocking your ears. Do owls even have ears?

Of course owls have ears! I can hear you, can't I?

36

COMING, MOM!
Well, I've got to go.
You heard Mom with your
weird little owl ears.
See ya later.
Bye now.

Bea . . . your mom
isn't calling.

37

I'm feeling pretty <YAWN> tired. Maybe I'll try tomorrow.

But we're skating today.

Oh well, I guess I'll miss out.

Hmm . . .

38

I think there's a secret here.

Nope. No secrets here.

Yep, it's the secret of what-is-really-going-on-with-Bea?

Are you afraid, Bea?

What? Me? No. Of course not. I'm not scared. Nope. Not me.

There's nothing to be afraid of. We wear these pads and it doesn't hurt at all if you fall.

Well, that's not what I'm afraid of. It's—

40

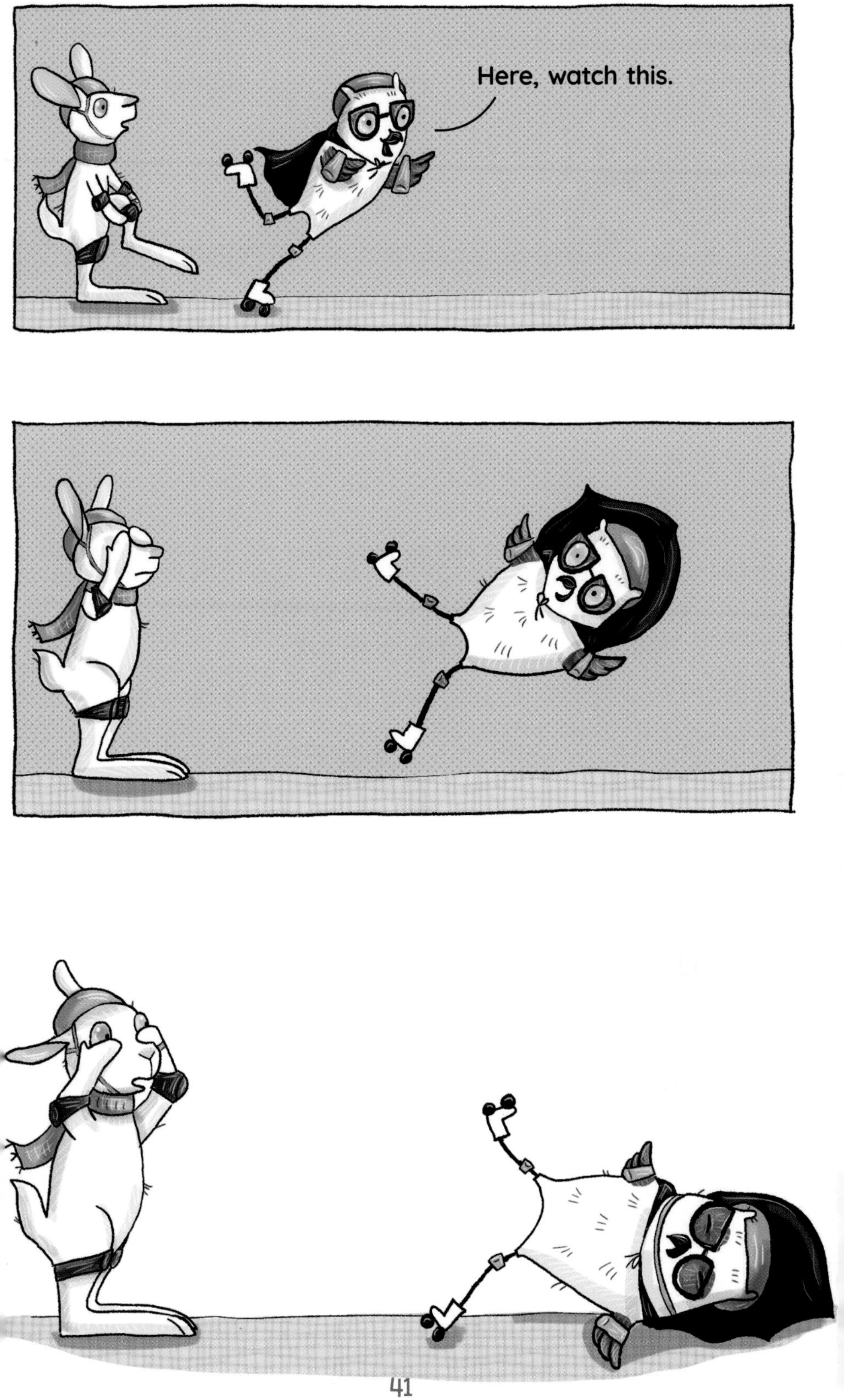
Here, watch this.

Ollie, are you okay?

Yep. My helmet keeps me safe.

SEE, YOU DON'T NEED TO BE AFRAID OF GETTING HURT.

Although the ground is still the hardest part!

42

Well . . .

I guess I am a little afraid . . .

but not of that.

What if I look silly? Well, sillier than I already do with my big feet?

43

It's okay to look silly.
Silly is fun.
Look!

See Simon!
He's so squirrelly!

I'm calling him
**SQUEALS ON
WHEELS!**

44

And CeeCee is *otter*-ly goofy!
And *oh, deer!*
Don't forget Sera or Pedro!
THEY ARE ONE IN *CHAMELEON!*

AND THEY ARE ALL HAVING FUN!!!

But I look silly because of my big feet. They look like snowmobiles on wheels.

WE'LL CALL THEM POLAR ROLLERS!!!

Sorry, Bea.

That's okay.

Hey, Bea, what's orange and sounds like a parrot?

I don't know.

A CARROT!

That's silly.

CHAPTER 5
YOU *OTTER* BE KIDDING ME

THAT'S IT!
I know how to solve this mystery!

This is still not a mystery.

I DON'T WANT TO SKATE!
I have huge feet and I don't want to look ridiculous!!!

But that's just it!
You shouldn't *carrot* all about looking ridiculous.

Hmpf. That *sounds* ridiculous.

IT IS RIDICULOUS!!!
You'll see! Wait right *hare.*
Owl be back!

LET'S GET SKATING!

You're a **bit funny.**

Well, you're a **fit bunny.** Now *hop* to it!

That's fine. *Owl* be back.

I'm not ready.

51

Bea, can you grab my book from under there?

Under where?

UNDERWEAR, INDEED!

52

Are you **ready to roll?**

Almost, but I still look sillier than you.

For the last time, *owl* be back.

53

Is someone having a **bad hair day?**

Or is it a BAD *HARE* DAY?

54

Are you ready now?

OKAY, OKAY, YES! YES! I'M READY NOW!

CHAPTER 6
IT'S *OWL* GOOD!

Hey, Bea!
Knock, knock!

Who's there?

Orange.

Orange, who?

ORANGE you glad we solved this mystery?

YES, I AM!!!

57

We are the **fast—**

And the *furriest!*

Don't forget the **silliest too!**

58

Ollie, everyone looks totally ridiculous.

I know, but it's fun, right?

Right?

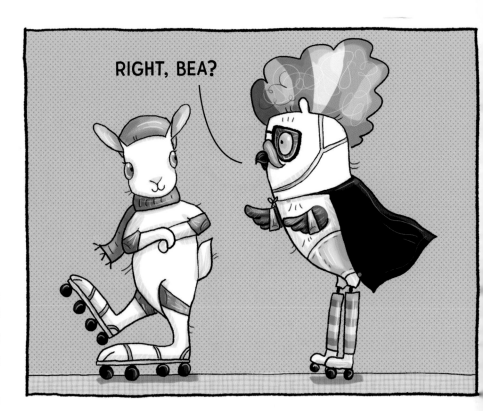

RIGHT, BEA?

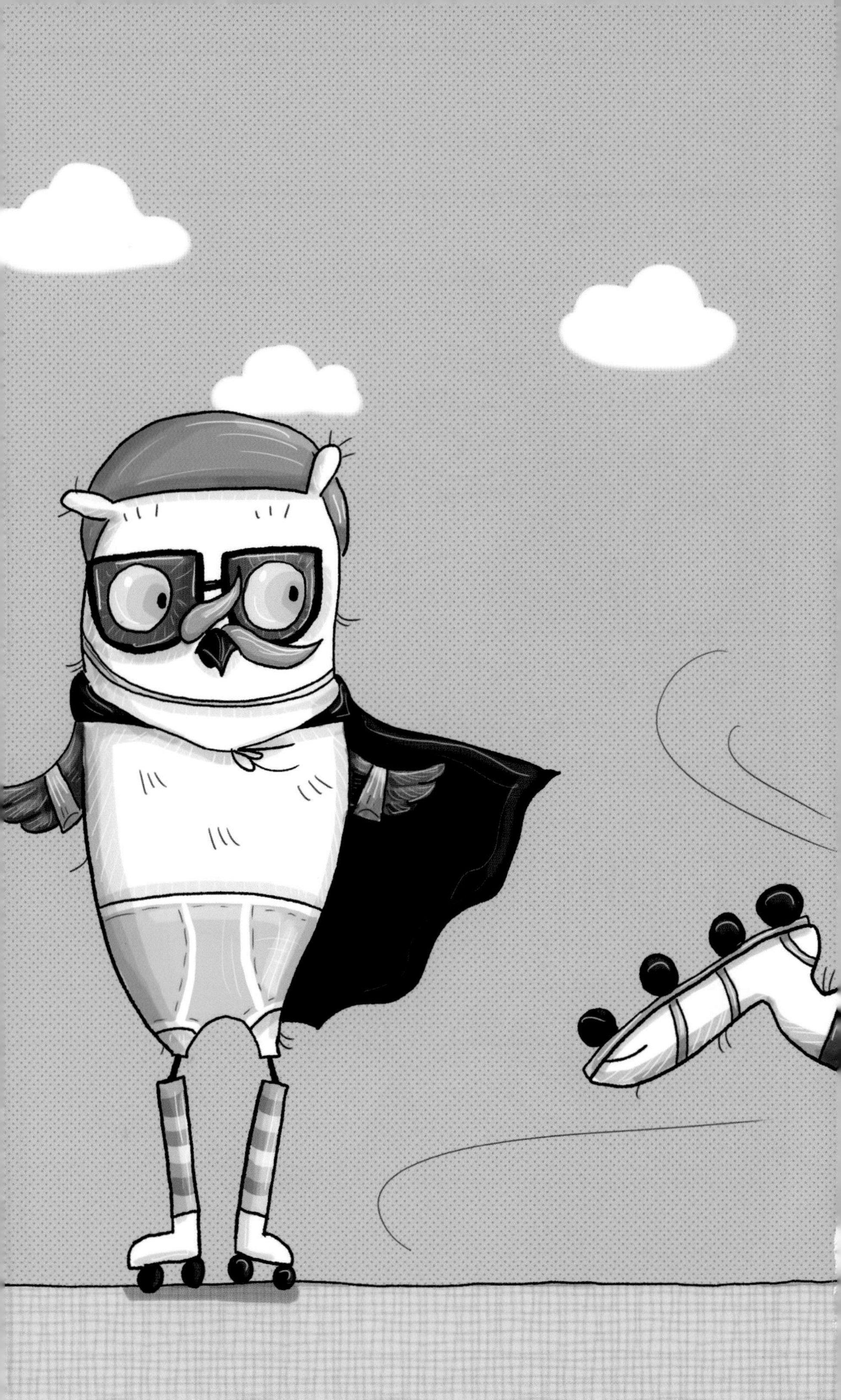

RIGHT!!!

LOOK AT THAT! ANOTHER *HOPPY* ENDING!

THAT'S *OWL*, FOLKS!

ABOUT THE CREATOR

Renée Treml was born and raised in the United States and now lives on the beautiful Surf Coast in Australia. Her stories and illustrations are inspired by nature and influenced by her background in environmental science. When Renée is not writing or illustrating, she can be found walking in the bush or on the beach, or exploring museums, zoos, and aquariums with her family and superenthusiastic little dog.